My Red Balloon

by
Eve Bunting

Illustrated by
Kay Life

Boyds Mills Press

Published by Boyds Mills Press, Inc.
A Highlights Company
815 Church Street
Honesdale, Pennsylvania 18431

Library of Congress Cataloging-in-Publication Data

Bunting, Eve, 1928-
My red balloon / by Eve Bunting ; illustrated by Kay Life.
    p. cm.
Summary: A young boy waits with both excitement and apprehension for
his father to disembark from the aircraft carrier returning to port
after many months at sea.
 ISBN 1-59078-263-1 (alk. paper)
 [1. Fathers and sons—Fiction. 2. Children of military personnel—Fiction.
3. United States. Navy—Fiction.]
I. Life, Kay, ill. II. Title.

PZ7.B91524My 2005
 [E]—dc22

                                        2004029200

First edition, 2005
The text of this book is set in 15-point Stone Serif.
The illustrations are done in watercolor.

10 9 8 7 6 5 4 3 2 1

For my daddy, who came home from a different war
                              —E. B.

*"Dedicated to the men and women who serve, and the families
who wait. . . ."* Special thanks to Sammy and VJ Comai and family,
Luana and family, and to Virginian Pilot *news photographer*
Martin Smith-Rodden.
                              —K. L.

THE FIRST THING I SEE when Mom wakens me is my red balloon that's shaped like a heart. On it is printed WELCOME HOME.

It's waiting.

Mom and I have been waiting, too.
But today's the day.
I jump out of bed and dress.

I bring my red balloon downstairs and twist the string around the arm of my chair. It floats above the table.

WELCOME HOME.

Mom is dressed real pretty. So am I. Even my Spiderman underpants are new.

Mom pours cereal, but we don't eat much.

"Will Daddy be happy to come home?" I ask.

"Very happy."

"But he had a job to do," I say. "Being on his ship. Making sure our country stays safe." I know this because I've asked before.

"That's right, Bobby." Mom kneels to tie my tennies.

My red balloon doesn't want to go in the car with us. We push it gently. It rises to the roof, its string attached to my wrist.

We see the crowds and the jammed-up parking lot before we get to the pier where the big ship will come in.

"Lots of daddies and mommies are coming home today," Mom says happily.

There sure are lots of people jostling around, big people, little people, even babies in strollers or tucked in those little sling things that hang from their mommies' shoulders. A band's playing real loud.

"Can you see it yet?" someone asks a tall, tall man.

"Not yet," he says.

"Your son's coming home?" the same someone asks.

"My daughter." The man smiles a huge smile that flashes out from under his mustache.

"My daddy's coming," I tell him, and I look up at my red balloon and jerk it so it bows. It's high above everyone, even the tall, tall man. After we meet him, my daddy always puts me up on his shoulders. If I were up on his shoulders now, my red balloon would touch the clouds.

The girl next to me tries to hold my balloon string, too, but I say: "Don't touch. This is for my daddy." She's bigger than I am.

I move to Mom's other side, just in case.

My red balloon is very important. Mom wrote to
Daddy and told him I'd be carrying a red balloon today.
I move it fast so it jumps and bounces.

Suddenly, there's an enormous cheer.

"There it is!" a man shouts.

I cheer, too, so loud it feels as if my ears are going to burst.

The big gray ship with the flat deck where airplanes can land and take off is coming. I can see the sharp-nosed planes and the tiny figures of the sailors lined up along the railing.

The band's playing extra loud now. I know the song. It's one of Daddy's. "Anchors Aweigh," which is OK even though the song's about a ship going out, not coming in.

We're all singing and clapping in time. A woman who looks like my grandma is giving out flowers from a humongous bunch she carries. But she's too far away from us. I guess we won't get one.

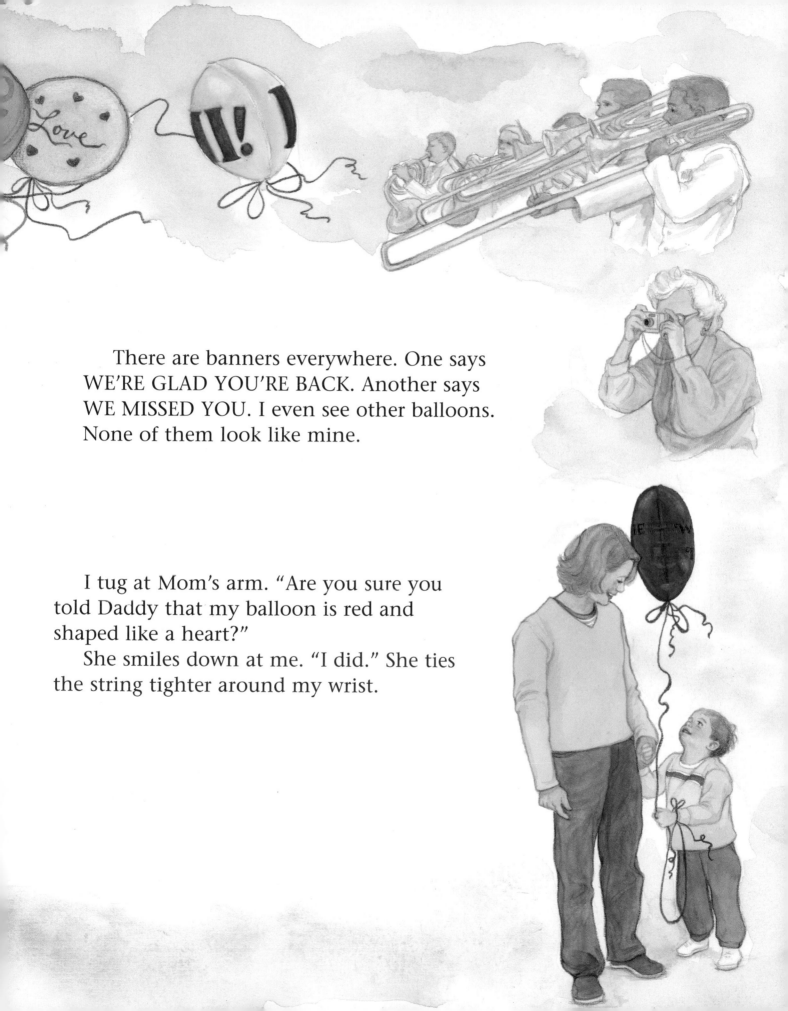

There are banners everywhere. One says WE'RE GLAD YOU'RE BACK. Another says WE MISSED YOU. I even see other balloons. None of them look like mine.

I tug at Mom's arm. "Are you sure you told Daddy that my balloon is red and shaped like a heart?"

She smiles down at me. "I did." She ties the string tighter around my wrist.

"Whew!" I mutter. Ever since Mom told me it was time for Daddy to come home again I've been worried. What if this time he doesn't recognize me? I think I'm a lot bigger. But now I have my red balloon shaped like a heart, and I'll be real easy to find.

The ship is gliding to a stop at the pier. Its deck is so far above us that it's like looking at a tall building. I can't tell which sailor is my daddy. From here they all look the same.

All around me people are jumping around, kissing and hugging. I hope no one hugs me except my mom.

She has tied the string
too tight. It's hurting my wrist.

I poke my finger under the loop to make it bigger, and it comes all the way loose. It's slipping out of my hand. Before I know what's happening, it floats away.

I watch it go up and up. I try to shout, but it doesn't come out right.

"Help!" I wail. "Mom! My balloon!"

My heart's punching inside of me.

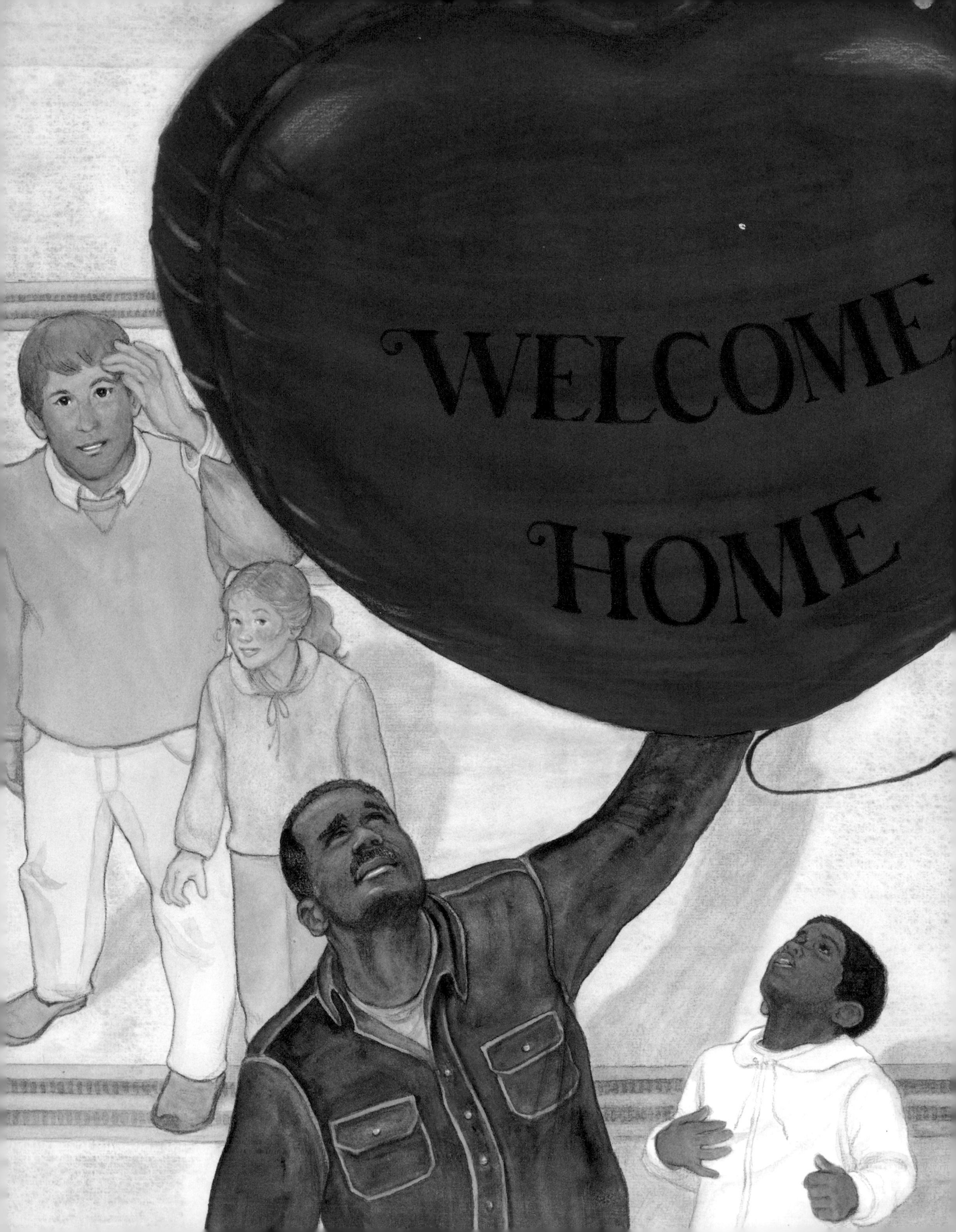
WELCOME
HOME

Mom looks up. "Oh no," she says. She jumps to try to catch the string, but already it's too high.

The tall, tall man sees it, and he jumps, too. He jumps another time. Then he says sadly, "I'm sorry, kiddo. I'm afraid it's gone."

We stand there, shading our eyes from the sun, watching my red balloon that's shaped like a heart dancing happily against the sky. Its long, skinny string sways beneath it.

My eyes are stinging.

Mom scrooches down beside me, and suddenly
I'm crying.

"Daddy won't know me," I whisper, and Mom says,
"What do you mean? He'll always know you. . . ."

Then a woman shouts "Little boy! Little boy! Look!
Look at your balloon."

I lift my head. My red balloon that's shaped like a heart has sailed across to the ship and is floating just above where the sailors are standing.

"See?" Mom says.

I stop sniffling.

And then I see my daddy. He's four from the end.

"Daddy! Daddy!" I yell.

Now all the men and women are rushing down from the ship, cramming, crunching into the crowd. And my daddy is beside us, kissing Mom, lifting me, holding me tight, and he's tall, tall, taller than anyone.

"Did you see my red balloon that's shaped like a heart?" I ask.

"Yes," he says. "I knew it was yours. Then I looked down here and I saw you."

"You did?"

He's giving me the best Daddy squeeze. I put my mouth close to his ear.

"Welcome home, Daddy."

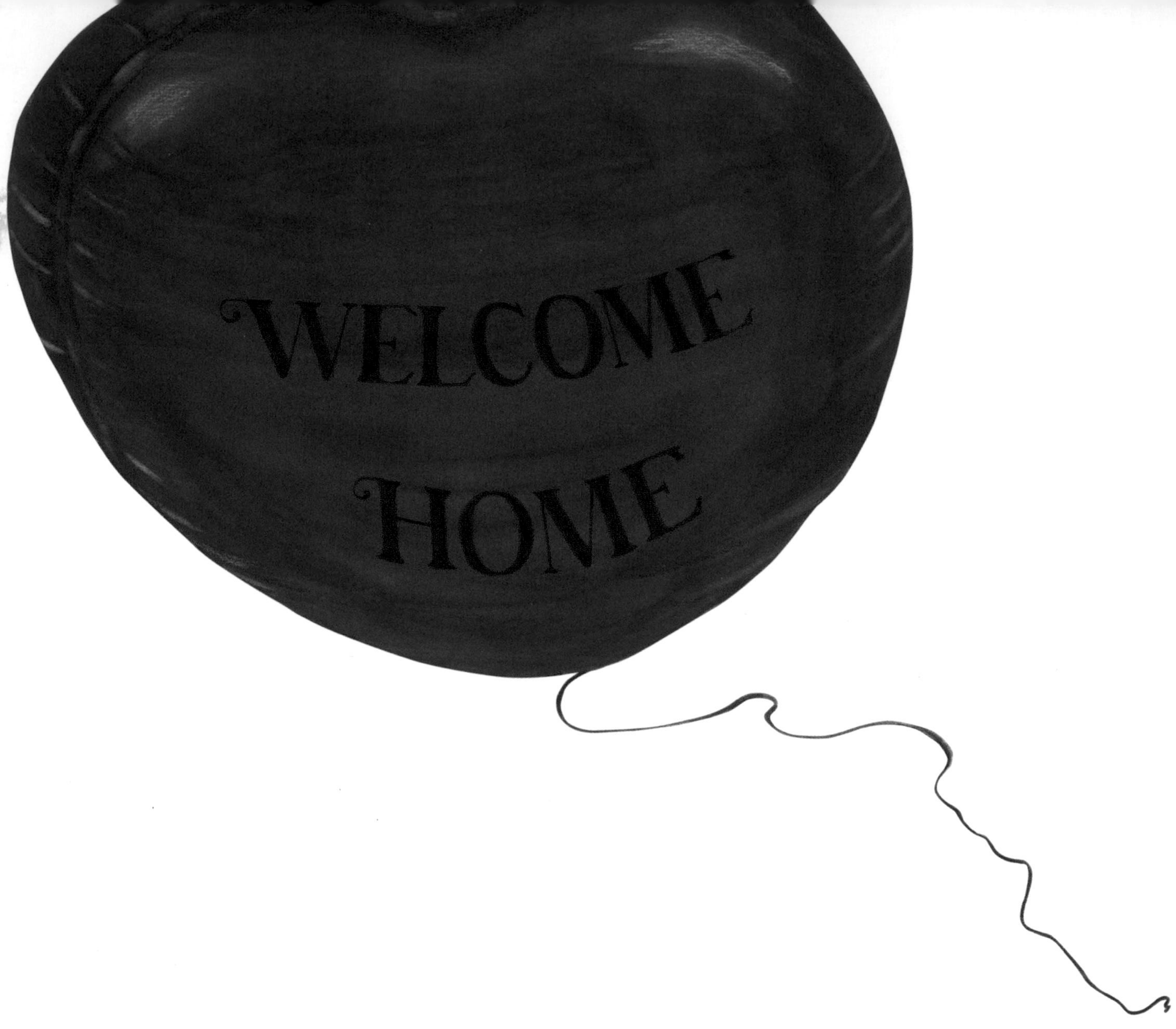
WELCOME
HOME